BUILDING HOPE

A NOVEL

MARIE F. BEARDWOOD

First Stillwater River Publications Edition

Library of Congress Control Number: 2019920945

ISBN-13: 978-1-950-33985-3

1 2 3 4 5 6 7 8 9 10
Written by Marie F. Beardwood
Cover design by Emma St. Jean
Cover photo by Anne Desrosiers ©2020
Published by Stillwater River Publications, Pawtucket, RI, USA.

Publisher's Cataloging-In-Publication Data
(Prepared by The Donohue Group, Inc.)

Names: Beardwood, Marie F., author.
Title: Building hope : a novel / Marie F. Beardwood.
Description: First Stillwater River Publications edition. | Pawtucket, RI,
    USA : Stillwater River Publications, [2020]
Identifiers: ISBN 9781950339853
Subjects: LCSH: High school girls--Rhode Island--Providence--Fiction. |
    Education, Secondary--Rhode Island--Providence--Fiction. | Educa-
    tional change--Rhode Island--Providence--Fiction. | High school
    students--Social conditions--Fiction.
Classification: LCC PS3602.E2552 B85 2020 | DDC 813/.6--dc23

The views and opinions expressed in this book are solely those of the author and do not necessarily reflect the views and opinions of the publisher.

DEDICATION

This book is dedicated to all of my students, but especially to Providence public school students. You have touched my life in so many ways, made me a stronger educator, and I treasure you and the richness you have brought to my life.

CHAPTER 1

I'm gonna tell you a story about a school. It was a mad crazy place at first, kids just comin' 'n goin' whenever they want and not much learning happening neither. There was gangstas and playahs and fights 'n stuff like that. But then some big politician got involved and it must've been an election year or something 'cause all of a sudden we're on that skinny white dude's radar. He's on the radio and TV telling everyone how he's gonna fix my school. Huh.

See, the school was bad. Graffiti and no supplies and stuff broken and students and teachers mostly not caring. Nobody going to school on time. Nobody learning nothing. One sorry math teacher put his fat legs up on his desk every day and read the paper and don't teach us nothing. No doors on the stalls in the bathrooms. What's a girl to DO if she needs to go???

But let me start at the beginning.

I was gonna go to high school! I was pretty excited, finally getting outta my dumb middle school.

You're supposed to have school choice in Providence, right? That's where I'm supposed to be able to pick the school that is right for me. As a LEARNER. All I know about myself as a LEARNER is I want to be TAUGHT. Maybe I should pick a school based on how those teachers are as TEACHERS???

Kind of a joke, tho', right? The way we learn about SCHOOL CHOICE is all messed up. First we have this ASSEMBLY where these ADMINISTRATORS announce SCHOOL CHOICE. But here's the thing. The SCHOOL that I CHOOSE has to be in my neighborhood. Huh. Some choices I got. So anyway these ADMINISTRATORS keep on talkin' 'n talkin' 'n flappin' their lips and we all get bored and restless and they say we are being DISRESPECTFUL. Then they say if we're INTERESTED we can go to these school choice EVENTS and these EVENTS will be held all over the city. Funny, why isn't there one of them events held in my neighborhood? If I want to go to one, I have to catch two buses to get over to the other side. I don't even know where those places are! I wonder if there is anyone that even LOOKS like me in those sections of town. Huh. I wonder what schools are like in THOSE neighborhoods?? Bet the schools in THOSE neighborhoods are clean and have doors on the bathroom stalls and fat old white men teachers don't put their fat old hairless legs up on their desks and don't teach NOTHING. I'll show you who is DISRESPECTING who. Lame ADMINISTRATORS.

So they give us all these FORMS that have to be filled out in a certain WAY or our choices will be INVALID. And when we return the forms to the STUDENT

REGISTRATION AND PLACEMENT CEN-
TER, we will be treated FAIR and EQUITA-
BLE. That means EQUAL. Think I get
treated the same as those rich kids on the
EAST SIDE??

I start to look at the forms in the fat
envelope and there are pages and pages and
pages and I ask myself how am I supposed
to do all this? And some of the stuff they ask
I wanna be RUDE when I write my answers,
like when they ask "Current location as res-
idence." Would under a BRIDGE count??
Seriously, my friend Shontelle's family keeps
having to MOVE because they can't pay the
RENT so they just jump from apartment to
apartment carrying their sorry clothes 'n
stuff in black plastic garbage bags 'n one
time they did end up under a bridge.

Later on, I go on the website to read
more 'cause I learned to NAVIGATE the
web and I find a quick reference guide, all
right. It is for REPORTERS. Where's my
quick reference guide???

I fill out all the forms and some of it
my daddy fills out when I can catch him
before he goes to sleep after his shift at the

hospital. I say which school I want to go to and I pick Classical because that is the best school in the city. You all got to be tested and pass some test to get in. I figured I didn't have no chance with that. But, a girl can always try, right?

So I fill out the forms 'n drop them off at the STUDENT REGISTRATION AND PLACEMENT CENTER. The lady behind the counter stands there double-checking my name, like I don't know how to spell or something. Listen here, Vanilla. Yeah, it is 'Seaira.' And don't go giving me that look like your name Heather is all that special. You named for a plant, ho.

Anyways, I got the forms filled out and she took it and put it in this big pile like I ain't special at all. Like I am just one more sorry student she got to deal with. So, I tried to find out when the test is and she give me all this attitude saying she will be "NOTIFYING" me at the "APPROPRIATE" time. Using these big words making me feel all stupid and bad about myself. And making me feel like I am one big inconvenience to her. It is her JOB to help me.

So I left there knowing I was not gonna get the school of my choice. Sorry process anyway. Although I do wonder what school I will go to but I guess I gotta wait and see.

And sure enough I did not get into Classical—got sent to a place called Hope clear across the city. They send me way over there even though all the LITERATURE says all this stuff about "neighborhood" schools. Hope ain't in my neighborhood at ALL. It is over three miles away! Maybe even three-and-a-half! How am I supposed to get way over there? ADMINISTRATION says I'm supposed to take the BUS. No yellow school bus either—I have to take PUBLIC TRANSPORTATION. The city gives bus passes for any student living at least three miles from their school. Just so you know, three miles is the longest "QUALIFYING DISTANCE" in the state. But that is a LONG way to walk. Long! A bunch of us protested 'n got the news to talk about our protest 'n us trying to get those fat politicians and ADMINISTRATORS to walk that three miles so they understand what three miles is. Different than sitting in your comfy car listening to music with the heat or the air conditioning on. Some of those politicians made that walk with us but it didn't matter. Qualifying distance is still qualifying distance. At least I get to take the bus 'n I don't have to walk. Man, those politicos should walk when it is WINTER and it has been SNOWING and nobody and I mean NOBODY shovels the sidewalks so we all gotta walk in the STREET and that is DANGEROUS let me tell you. People get hit ALL the time. It is a law and everything that you SUPPOSED to shovel but why is that law not ENFORCED? And let me just point out that the EAST SIDE? Nobody protested from THAT neighborhood. Maybe they all get their sidewalks taken care of. Or maybe there are NO WALKERS. Probably have their mommies drive them. Or they have their own cars. Poor babies.

Anyways! Hope. Ha. That is funny to call a school that. Lots of us call it "hopeless." Because it is one sorry place. Seems a lot of kids that go there don't graduate and don't do nothin' with their sorry selves. Some do, but I hear they had to scratch and claw their way to accomplishing something. I heard too that sometimes that fancy college right near Hope gives a free ride to one kid from Hope. Just one, tho'. Guess that's about as generous as they can afford. Huh.

CHAPTER 2

So I go to the school on the first day and there's some kids I know there. Like Javona and Carlos and Gerry and Aaron and Shontelle and a few others. I get on that bus the first day 'n have to pay because I don't have my bus pass yet 'n get over to school. They pack us in like sardines on that bus 'cause there's so many of us. Sign on the wall says the legal capacity is forty and just because I don't feel like talking to nobody, I count and we're waaaay over that number. Packed in just like those sardines. In oil. Some of you people need to take a SHOWER and not use so much oil. All of us crammed against one another. Some of the lucky ones got seats; everybody else got to stand. And the sign says no one standing beyond some line at the front of the bus for the safety of the passengers. Yeah, well I can't even see no line. Safety. HA.

So we drive up this big steep hill and over to the East Side. I been here before. There's a big university here called Brown—that's the one that gives a free ride to one Hope kid a year—and some fancy private school. I can see that fancy school through the trees with the grass all green and a bunch of girls with their long blonde hair carrying some lacrosse sticks or field hockey sticks. Riiiiight. Field hockey. 'N the houses are huge, all painted fancy with fancy cars in the driveways. Who needs a house that big anyhow? What do you all do in a house that big? With bathrooms and bedrooms and sitting areas and eating areas. I been in one of those houses once and there's not one, not two, but three places to eat! Eat-in-kitchen they call it. Where else you supposed to eat?? Then there's this formal dining room with fancy chairs and fancy table. Even a breakfast nook. A what? That is mad crazy. Just park yourself down and eat!

So we arrive at the school and all of us get off the bus and cross the road, takin' our time and cross any which way and totally pissin' off the drivers of them fancy cars trying to get to work on time 'cuz they need to be taking care of BUSINESS. But we stroll across the street just to piss them off until this big tall black guy—he's the principal with a crew cut—starts yellin' at us, "Come on, PEOPLE! Let's GO!" Like just because he's hollering at us we gonna be picking up the pace. Yeah, right, mister. We're gonna get there when we get there.

So they herd us all into this auditorium with its big high ceilings. The roof is in some sorry state. There are pigeons flying up above. So we get our schedules, but it is a loooong disorganized process trying to give a thousand or so students their new schedules. I know there are over a thousand of us because the fire sign says "Capacity 2000" and the place is half full. By the time I get my schedule it is almost lunch as they go in alphabetical order and my last name is Williams.

So, they tell us how to read the schedule and we are supposed to go to our third period class but forget THAT—eh it is the first day and I'm hungry so I'm gonna go to lunch. But, I get to the cafeteria for some of that sorry food and I don't got no money, but I find out I can get free lunch if I go to my third period class to get my free lunch card, so I sigh and go to my third period class.

So I walk in late and they've already passed out all the lunch cards so I ask what am I supposed to do and the teach, she say well go to the office, so I go to the office and there is a big long line of students whining and moaning they didn't get no lunch card. So I gotta decide am I gonna wait and get a lunch card? Will tomorrow be easier to get a lunch card? What if I go to the cafeteria and just take food? I decide I am gonna go to the caf and try and get food that way. So I go back down and I am hungry and I get in line and it is mad crazy down there and the lunch ladies are losing it a little because there's kids everywhere. I am able to grab me a couple of pieces of pepperoni pizza and a milk. Pizza is soggy and cold but I eat it anyway. I sit with Nieva and some other ho I don't know and it is mad crazy around us. Kids everywhere on their phones and playin' music and talkin' and laughin' and throwin' food. And then the bell rings and it is time to go to our fourth period class. I already hate that bell. I am not a dog that just responds to some bell.

I go to find my fourth period class. And it is Miz Anna and she's all right, I can tell right from the start. She starts by making sure she knows all our names. She even wants us to sit in certain seats so she can make a SEATING CHART. She's not any new teach either. She's got grey hair and all and says she gonna teach us English. Some of the kids start jiving and talking trash 'n saying stuff like, "What, you don't think we can speak English?" and that got everybody started, hollering about being DISRESPECTED. But, Miz Anna, she was polite 'n respectful 'n calm, calling those boys "mister" and the girls "miss" so we kind of settled down, especially as she was telling us this class isn't about English 'n how to SPEAK it, but about stories. And right away she pulled out this story by a brother by the name of Richard Wright 'n reads us some 'n we get all quiet 'n listen. She makes sure everybody gets a copy of that book 'n that's what we're going to do in that class to start. Seems like that will be alright with everybody.

Then the bell rings again. I hate that bell, it is so loud like my dead grammie could hear it. But even though Miz Anna is trying to say stuff about homework we are out the door.

The hallways are mad crazy with kids yellin' and runnin' and talkin' trash. There's a couple of kids fighting over something—I don't know WHAT—and a couple of these sorry teachers walk by and don't even pay it no never mind though one of them kids is bleeding from his head. They're afraid I bet. I'm a little afraid too as I see these neck pieces on those niggas and know it is some kind of gang ACTIVITY they are getting into in the halls.

That big black guy with the crew cut is hollerin' again, "Let's go people!" like we're a bunch of goats or sheep or dogs and we're just gonna to do what he says. But it is a nice day out 'n the school day is so over so we wanna get out of that smelly old building anyways, so we head on out.

Bunch of us are just hanging around the front of the school. There's some more kids I know 'n one guy I kind of like, so we talk. He starts tossing little pebbles at me 'n at my junk 'n I know he's liking me a bit too, but I can't hang I gotta get home 'cuz my little brother from another mother needs someone home to take care of him. My daddy won't get home 'til late after he finishes his shift up at the hospital. So I head on out thinking, well, another lame year has started.

CHAPTER 3

The next day I get up 'n get my brother dressed 'cuz my daddy is still sleepin' from the long night at the hospital. So I gotta get us off to school, 'n my brother's school starts later than mine, but I gotta get him there, see? So I get him there and make sure he takes the right bus and show him how to go 'cuz I am hoping that he's gonna be able to do that for his sorry self so I don't have to walk him to the door every day like I am his mama.

So, of course this makes me late to get to my school 'n they're all pissed off at me, but what the hey people? A girl's got OBLIGATIONS, baby. Stuff I gotta DO, you know? But they just don't wanna hear it. I get detention for my "TARDINESS" 'n I get some sorry piece of paper 'n the vanilla behind the counter tells me I gotta get to school on time 'n where to go for detention 'n I better be there too because there will be "RAMIFICATIONS." 'N I was gonna start to get up in her cold face but her hard eyes stop me. Eyes ice blue. Even her name is hard, "Crystal," and I take my stupid slip and walk away 'n go to my first class late.

And I get to my first class late with my slip that says the lame teacher has to let me in 'n he does, but he gives this big sigh like the weight of the world is on his shoulders, and I wanna say you think YOU have the weight of the world on YOUR shoulders???? Who is gonna pick up my brother from another mother this afternoon while I sit in some room to punish me for something I ain't got no control over?!?! But I don't say nothing, just take the math book he gives me and find a seat in the front 'cuz all the back seats are taken.

All those kids in the back of the room are acting just too cool for school all laid out like that. Their big old feet blocking the path and slouching with their pants low so I can see their sorry underwear or the crack of their butts, thinking they're so cool with their hats on sideways, and some of them wearing shades and grinning like fools flashing their grills. They're some sorry kids trying to act like men but really are boys. I know they are not gonna last long; they'll come when it is cold 'n when they are hungry or bored. They're just showing who's who and what's what is all. Letting everybody know who is in charge.

CHAPTER 4

That's the way it is. Same bull day in 'n day out. And I get so weary of the bull and most of the teachers not caring and the crappy food and the fights. Just dog tired from the bull. Man. But I kept going through the motions and feeling more 'n more tired 'n like nobody cares, 'n everybody around me failing this and failing that and no hope. That's the funny part. No Hope.

CHAPTER 5

Like, the other day we're sitting in science class and the teach Dr. Ramirez is doing his thing with whatever he is trying to show us but he ain't got a lot of equipment and he keeps saying stuff like, "If I had this piece of equipment, I could show you," so I guess we got to IMAGINE our education and what we're supposed to be learning.

Dr. Ramirez is cool, tho', he's all right. He was a doctor in the Dominican Republic. A full doctor, you know, that can look down people's throats. But when he came to this country the ESTABLISHMENT didn't like his CREDENTIALS and won't let him be el medico so he got a teaching certificate so he can educate us.

But life is a little lame in that classroom 'n as much as we like Dr. Ramirez, life needs to be LIVENED UP. So these two playahs start going at it a bit, just trashing at each other, 'til one of 'em mentions the other guy's MOTHER—man, never mention the other guy's mother unless you want to get INTO it. And sure enough they do and the CONFRONTATION gets bigger and spills out into the hallways and doors open 'n next thing you know you got full scale STUFF on your hands.

So somebody calls the cops 'cuz this spilled right out the front doors right on to Hope Street and kids everywhere kicking 'n punching 'n showing weapons. You know, flashing a knife or them brass knuckles. Lots of us just tried to keep out of the way 'cause we don't want no part of THAT. But we stay to watch the action, you know?

And sure enough some black vans with "GANG UNIT" on the side come screaming up and news cameras start rolling and I think this is gonna make the news. And the "GANG UNIT" doors open and these muscle-headed white boys get their sorry selves outta that van thinking they're gonna be breaking this up, but don't they know their PRESENCE alone is just pissing us off?? First they're looking like FOOLS all dressed in black with all this stuff swinging from their waists. Handcuffs and clubs and tasers and so much dangling there it is a wonder they can even MOVE. 'N second, they're white boys. No cracker is gonna be tellin' these niggas to settle down. 'N they're all strutting around the place trying to "MAINTAIN CONTROL" and handcuffing the brothahs 'n even a few sistahs. It takes a good long while for the place to quiet down. White lady across the way in one of those fancy houses is outside holding her sweater closed at her throat like we're gonna slice that throat wiiiiide open and rob her or something. I kinda wanna just holler at the honkey just to scare her. But I don't.

'N sure enough, that night when my daddy watched the late news he comes in

to my bedroom to ask me what happened,
woke me up even—he was that worried—'n
I tell him 'n he just sighs 'n lays a hand on
my head 'n prays for my safety. I feel safest
and loved when my daddy does that for me.

CHAPTER 6

Another time I know this teach was tapping a student. She's all thick and showing herself as she's walking down the hall as if nobody is noticing that she is advertising herself 'n she took to hugging this kid Aaron who is in the 11th grade. A SIDE hug, because that is a SAFE hug. But we all know that a hug is a hug and hugs can lead to other things. It is a body touching a body, right? And sure enough, Miz H starts to offer Aaron extra help a lot, 'n that's funny 'cause nobody but nobody offers anybody ANY extra help around here, and I guess Aaron really likes the extra help cause he's going for it a lot. Gerry 'n some of the other playahs like to wait 'til Aaron goes in the room with Miz H 'n they slide on up to that classroom door 'n look through the window 'n watch the goings on. Heard they got themselves some vid-eeee-oooo. Huh, wonder what they gonna do with that!?

CHAPTER 7

In math class, the teach starts talking about a test we gotta take to see where we are ACADEMICALLY and I hate that they are always testing us. Why don't you test me on how to take care of my little bro and feed my daddy with the little bit of green he gives me every week? Yeah. That's some MATH.

So the teacher keeps talking and talking and talking on and on about the kneecap and I'm thinking to myself KNEE-CAP? But then he writes it on the board the NECAP and all those letters mean something, but I can't really remember.

Except the A is for ASSESSMENT. All I know is the teacher keeps saying we have to do good on this test. Can't help but wonder why do we have to do good on this test? I'm pretty sure the RESULTS will be more about the EDUCATIONAL SYSTEM than they are about ME and MY EDUCATION.

So he teaches and he teaches and he teaches all this stuff with all these math symbols and the stupid playahs in the back is just being a disTRACtion and everybody not paying that teacher no never mind.

And all the other classes are talkin' 'bout that sorry test. Test just made up by the BUREAUCRACY and THE MAN to show just how stupid we are 'n how great those blonde kids over at that fancy school are. Sigh.

'N sure enough, those test results come back and everybody is all in an uproar about Hope being the worst school in the state. Man, I coulda told you THAT. Saved you some money, too. Just come on in half my classes and see how much we're prepared to take some fancy test. Asking me about PORCUPINES and why they don't have to fight. Having to write an ESSAY. When you ever seen a porcupine in the city? When have you ever seen a porcupine fight? I didn't even know what a porcupine WAS! Why don't you ask me about STRATEGIES I use to fight ADMINISTRATORS every day about being late? That is a subject I can write on.

And then telling me to use a THESAURUS. What is THAT?

And asking me about some blue ice CREVASSE—are you kidding me I didn't even know what ice was 'til I got in this country and almost froze to death the first winter here. All I had was a sweater and I damn near froze. My skin all ashy 'n dry. My lips so cracked they kept bleeding. My hands cracked too 'cause I didn't have no gloves.

Another part of that test is about writing and it asked me to write about helping a new student have lunch in your school cafeteria for the first time. I have to write a procedure explaining how to "successfully survive" the experience. Survive.

Yeah, that's funny. I'll show you how to survive. First you steal the new kid's lunch card and then you lose yourself in the crowd right quick and then come back later and use the lunch card to get your free sorry lunch. Or just wait 'til some of those lunch ladies aren't even looking 'n just slide on in 'n grab yourself a sorry tuna sandwich. Same question ask me to use "bullets" to help the reader. Huh, how 'bout if I pop you with a bullet, how's that, cracker? Is that what you mean by bullet?

'N I don't even wanna TALK about that math test. Letters meaning numbers, and shading 'n patterns. And which color line matches y=2x. Why don't you ask that fat lame white old math teacher who puts his legs up on the desk everyday 'n don't teach us NOTHIN' why we can't answer those questions? Huh? Ask HIM.

The one that cracked me up the most though was the EXCERPT from *Little Women* by Louisa May Alcott. The part where these girls are complaining how DREADFUL it is to be poor and how UN-FAIR life is when some girls have PRETTY dresses and other girls ain't got NOTHIN' at all. We supposed to identify main THEMES. I got a theme for you. This test is crazy 'n how are we supposed to compare to other schools in the state?? Especially as we ain't been taught NOTHING.

The whole school just about bug-eyed crazy over that test. Principal worrying over his reputation as a leader of a FAILED SCHOOL. That's KIDS you're talking about. Not a FAILED SCHOOL but FAILED KIDS. Teachers just saying these kids ain't never gonna pass, they don't learn, and why bother. And all the kids scratching themselves 'n giving up cause they know they ain't never gonna do good. Not ever. How'd them blonde girls do on that test?

Cracker test.

And it was all over Facebook and stuff—everybody all saying that Hope is the worst performing school in the state. Say what? You think we gonna compare ourselves to that blond-haired place a few blocks away? Yeah riiiight. But them news people keep showing up; photographers and pretty white boys with makeup right outside saying this and that about us and Hope High School. They wear MAKEUP! All blush and eye makeup. So while all this is going on about Hope and it being the worst school EVER, life goes on, man, you know?

We keep going to class to IMAGINE our education in science. And sleep in another class 'cuz that sorry excuse for a teach is putting his feet up on the desk every day. Put the newspaper over his face like we don't know what he's doing. The paper is MOVING, dawg. It's moving every time he SNORES! That is crazy. And we keep failing classes and subjects and not learning nothing.

CHAPTER 8

A kid who goes to school here died. Duka. Let me tell you about that. He was a "special ed" kid and had something wrong with him. I don't know what all it was. Sometimes the sickness is inside a body where you can't see it, you know? He was in special ed and sometimes seemed all far away when he was in the hallway or wherever. Just seemed all spacy or whatever. But whatever was going on, it was obvious to everybody that he was getting sicker 'n sicker. He kept spacing out and then he started walking funny. So he had to go to the hospital for an operation and he had some kind of ALLERGIC REAC-TION to the stuff that knocks you out. That doctor came out from surgery, the front of his green doctor's outfit all red with Duka's blood, telling the family that there were "COMPLICATIONS" and he got sick from the ANESTHESIA and was in a coma and was probably going to die. Doctor didn't even sit his sorry self down to talk to the family. He told them in front of EVERY-BODY in the waiting area and even gave them the news standing up, and even looked at his watch. Did not even give them five minutes of his time when their baby was probably gonna die. It was a sorry day.

I know Duka wanted to get the surgery 'cause he did not want to live like that no more. He told me that once when we was in a class together. He was special ed and all but took some regular classes with me. He just didn't want to live like that no more—all spaced out and not thinking right and walking funny sometimes. So he decided to have the surgery and now he's hanging on not alive and not dead. And his mother and father don't live together no more and they start fighting over their boy. Seems mom wants to "pull the plug" and let her baby die because he will never be the same 'n the QUALITY OF LIFE will be gone. He will pretty much be a vegetable, just lying there needing help breathing and probably having to have someone change his diaper for the rest of his life. The father doesn't want to PULL THE PLUG. He wants his son ALIVE. I get that, but is he really alive if he can't talk, can't move, can't run, just lays there and takes up space?? That hit the news too. Private pain being displayed for all to see. And Duka's brother still going to school, but like someone ripped out his heart 'cause his twin brother is lying in the hospital all curled up and hooked up to these machines and not living and not dying.

'N they start these court fights about what should happen with Duka and he's a HUMAN BEING, so how can you be putting his life like that on the news like his family ain't feeling like they've all got holes in their hearts from sadness? And then this judge is ruling and that judge is ruling and there are APPEALS and in the middle of all

that fighting Duka dies. I never really un-
derstood law before, but I think I understand where the word APPEAL comes from.

Sixteen years old and Duka dies.

And the funeral was in another city
'n we all had to ride on those smelly public
buses to get clear across to that big
church. And people assume that because
we are all young and brown that he died
from a gunshot or fight or some such
GANG-RELATED ACTIVITY or other VIO-
LENCE, but we know he didn't. We're all
dressed up—some of us even went to the
Salvation Army or the church to find a nice
shirt or dress or jacket and we are all just
ripped with sadness. Together we get off
the bus and we are kind of circled around
Duka's twin brother, supporting him and
just letting him know we are there for him.
And we wait in silence as they unload the
casket to bring it in to church and the up-
pity vanillas walking by us on the sidewalk
shake their heads in judgment as we are
waiting on his body. Tsk tsk is the noise
they make. Like they know the score. I
HATE YOU. YOU DON'T KNOW NOTHING.

And none of them teachers came from school to watch that kid be buried. It was school vacation and nobody heard, I guess. Can't imagine they were that stone cold to not even come. But imagine that? A boy from the school died and not one teach came.

His twin brother got himself a tattoo of his brother's name on his arm so every day he can look at that name 'n be reminded of him and his loss. Big block letters, like a prison tat. Why would a body want to do that, anyway? Be reminded of a loss like that. My momma died 'n I don't need no tattoo to remind me there's a hole in my heart every day.

CHAPTER 6

Another time there's this girl named Nia who never went to school or if she did, she never went to class. And the truancy officer finally got ahold of her and made Nia go to court to explain her BEHAVIOR. There's a courtroom right in Hope, you believe that? 'N once a week they put out these chairs along the hallway so families and kids have a place to sit while they wait for their APPEARANCE. 'N this judge comes in and there's a high bench in that room and the American flag and everything. 'N he sits up there like he is the LORD of the LAND, like he is God himself about ready to hand down JUDGMENT. Nia is totally screwed because she had been MIA for so long, the judge has to figure out a way to BREAK her and make her see the ERROR OF HER WAYS. That judge is evil, man. I do not ever want to see inside that cat's heart as it must be black as night in there.

The judge tells Nia she has to remove her extensions!! What the hey? What gives this judge the right to tell anybody to change their do?? Man that is just WRONG. Nia is really upset because she's got this long straight black hair that she has all neatly braided and it is her pride. You can tell she spent a lot of time and money on it—gorgeous extensions hanging right down her back all shiny and cared for. Can't that judge see that? Taking out those extensions would DESTROY Nia. Just hurt her where she lives. Might as well just cut the pride right out of that girl. But maybe the judge CAN see that. Maybe that's why's the judge is making her do that? Nia ain't never had but one thing that makes her proud, but one thing she can

call her own, right? 'Cause she got NOTH-
ING at home. This judge had all kinds of
things that his mommy 'n his daddy gave
his rich white boy self. He don't know
NOTHIN' about Nia and where she's been
and where's she's gonna go.

So Nia is all upset because if she
DON'T change her hair, that judge would
send her sorry self down to juvie and that
ain't no day camp you know what I'm saying? That is JUVIE man, and that is JAIL
for kids.

Or so I hear as I never been to juvie.
I don't want to make my daddy sad if I get
in enough trouble to get sent to JUVIE.

Anyways, Nia starts talking to anybody who will listen about her hair and
what that judge is making her DO and the
teach says you got to do what the judge
says. If you go ignoring that judge, you will
pay. There will be CONSEQUENCES for
your BEHAVIOR. So Nia thought on it 'n
just about busted herself UP trying to figure this one out, find a solution, but she
just couldn't, so she did it. She took out
her extensions and she was left with a

frizzy nappy head of hair. It looked awful. And you could see she knew it looked awful. It was a sad thing to see that girl with her head down 'n her shoulders all hunched over like the weight of the world was on her shoulders. And the teach kept saying that the ESTABLISHMENT sets the rules 'n you got to PLAY BY THE RULES 'n Nia BROKE THE RULES.

So after Nia removed her extensions, she went back to see the judge 'n the judge just kind of grunted at Nia and then that wasn't even enough for the judge! Nia's hair was too messy and didn't show a lick of pride, judge said and Nia had to do something about that to make herself PRESENTABLE. Man, didn't that judge see that the extensions WERE presentable?? And showed pride in herself?

So poor Nia had to go to a salon and get her hair cut and straightened and styled and pretty much had most of the sistah taken right out of her. That judge is pure evil, man. Not understanding a black girl's hair and what it means and applying his vanilla standards to her. Don't that judge got to go to training or anything so he shows he got some understanding of people and their SITUATIONS?? Guess not.

So Nia went again to the court in Hope and AGAIN that judge just grunted at her. He didn't even say nothin' about all her efforts. Man, I hate him. And I hate the system that just keeps us down.

But Nia was given a STAY OF EXE-CUTION 'n was allowed to stay with her family and to stay in school instead of going to juvie.

And after that, you could just see that the life was squeezed right out of her eyes and heart. That hair was her PRIDE and was about the only thing that belonged just to NIA. I ain't never been to her house, but if her life is anything like other kids here then she probably don't have her own bed or her own clothes and that hair gave her a sense of PRIDE. See?? It seemed to say. I DO CARE. I care about myself and how I look to people. But that judge didn't see that. All that white cracker saw was a homie being DISRESPECTFUL. 'N all that white cracker wanted to do was BREAK someone's back and heart and soul and spirit. You call yourself a judge. Let me tell you, YOU are no judge. You couldn't judge the QUALITY of a person or the FACTORS that impact a person to save your own white skin. Did you even THINK to ASK WHY Nia was never in school??? There are FACTORS that are impacting her SUCCESS. Stupid cracker.

I don't know. Nia did start to go to class but she was a shell. It was like a ghost had taken over. Was that what the judge wanted??? To break a body so completely? Maybe it was what he wanted, but why? What purpose did that serve?

CHAPTER 10

Another time there was a kid who was doing the same stuff as Nia—not going to class and causing problems and sometimes fighting. Judge asks to see the mother, so the mother's got to take time out of her job to catch a bus to come see the judge, and he keeps her waiting out in the hallway, taking his own sweet time to talk to her. Talk about being disrespected! And the mother is waiting and waiting and looking at her watch and knowing that every fifteen minutes is a little bit more of lost green for her family but what's a mother to do??? She was

ORDERED TO APPEAR so she APPEARED. And finally honky judge calls her in like she is a dog that should come on command, but she does and he does not even get down from his high bench to actually have a CONVERSATION with her. He just speaks at her from up in his high place and tells her all she is doing wrong as a mother. Does not ask her any questions or anything about the RESOURCES she needs to be successful, just LECTURES her on how awful she is. And the mother knows not to sass back. The mother has been around, I can tell you. She has seen the inside of a courtroom before. Or maybe she is just used to being told how awful she is by vanilla. So she says nothing and they agree to a plan. But AGREE isn't right. Judge says the plan and she nods because what is she going to do???? 'N the reason I know all this is because cracker leaves the door open to the hearing room so he can just humiliate anyone that has to appear before him. He don't give anyone no privacy at all.

And I watch her leave and she says thank you to the judge and her eyes are shuttered, because if her eyes showed what was in her head and in her heart, oh boy, she would have been in a world of trouble.

'N then it hit the news that this COURT was ILLEGAL! Imagine that! Some vanilla judge doing something illegal. So this big legal group called the ACLU got all up in the school's face 'n called out the JU-DICIAL SYSTEM and this group says the school can't go doing that. ACLU can do that. Don't know what all those letters mean, but they defend people against all kinds of stupidity. Anyway that group says you can't have no HEARING without the PROCEEDINGS being RECORDED. Man nothing was EVER recorded. And the students didn't get offered any REPRESENTA-TION ever. All over Facebook and stuff saying how kids were sent to juvie for NONAT-TENDANCE and that was no juvie offense. NO EFFORT WAS MADE TO DETERMINE THE CAUSE OF THE STUDENTS' TRU-ANCY. Huh. You surprised that no effort was made to DETERMINE THE CAUSE OF THE STUDENTS' TRUANCY? I ain't.

But they stopped those hearings. Good. Vanillas always sayin' what's best for us. Vanilla don't know. Vanilla don't struggle. Vanilla only ADDS to the struggle.

CHAPTER 11

One time, we had an OUTBREAK of some DISEASE.

So we're all in class. Not learning nothin' as usual, when the principal gets on to make an ANNOUNCEMENT over the PUBLIC ADDRESS SYSTEM that we got a case of that skin disease at Hope. I found out later it was called mersa but spelled MRSA. Anyways, the school's got this case of MRSA and it is HIGHLY CONTAGIOUS 'n we have to wash our hands THOROUGHLY after touching this 'n touching that 'n especially after going to the bathroom 'cause this disease is a flesh-eating thing like it came from outer space. Freaks people out, ya know? Principal ain't even finished with his AN-NOUNCEMENT when kids start screaming that they're gonna die. Other kids saying no man, this is that sickness where we gotta wear those face masks like some people do in China or Japan or wherever. Kids flipping open cellphones 'n calling parents 'cause they're scared 'n the principal is still speaking over the public address system, and you can hear the office phones ringing in the background over the intercom because just like that kids call moms and moms call the school and the place goes crazy. Classroom doors bust open—we ain't staying in school if we're gonna DIE right? So we leave. Spill outta classrooms into hallways 'n talking on the phone, some girls crying 'n principal saying over the public address system "calm down people" 'n that big tall black guy yelling at us AGAIN—what is up with that dude and all his yelling? Why can't he ever just ASK us something!? Instead of doing all that hollering? Christ on a crutch.

Next day we get a letter to take home that explains how to PREVENT THE

SPREAD of this FLESH EATING BACTE-RIA. That is just creepy.

'N they close the school to DECON-TAMINATE. They are gonna wash down every surface so students can safely return to school. Huh. Every surface, HA. You think they are gonna wash down every desk top? Every chair? Every DOOR-KNOB?? You know how big that school is??? Huh.

CHAPTER 12

In the middle of all this drama, the message is still that Hope is a FAILING SCHOOL. TEST SCORES ARE LOW. All them ADMINISTRATORS and POLITICIANS are arguing 'n pointing fingers. You think they actually cared with all that carrying on. Huh, the only thing they care about is their sorry selves. Those butts are on the LINE now. That's why they care.

And that's when they made all the changes.

But let me back up.

Ok, Hope is failing, they all say. What to do, what to do?? They all ask themselves and rub their hands like they are all really worried. Sure you are. Worried about your job.

They come up with this idea that Hope is too big and needs to be broken up. We got a little fired up over that—as much as Hope is lame, it is still OUR school and we have gotten to know it and we don't want to start over at another school. But what they mean is that they want to DIVIDE the school into separate LEARNING COMMUNITIES. Apparently RESEARCH SAYS that small learning communities, "lead to increased attendance, decreased dropout rates, more personalization, higher test scores." I'm pretty sure that GOOD TEACHERS would lead to the same thing, but what do I know? I'm just a kid.

They decided that they want three learning communities at Hope: Information Technology, Arts, and Leadership.

We're all like, riiiiight. Sure. You go ahead and develop those three learning communities. It is still gonna be the same old same old. Just like it is now. I just keep on going to class and it is same, same, same, old, old, old, every day.

But then stuff starts to HAPPEN. I hear they hire three new principals and three new assistant principals to LEAD each of those communities. More of those fancy news reporter boys with the makeup are in front of the school again. Everybody all flappin' and flappin' their lips over these CHANGES. Guess one of the biggest problems is something called a union. Teach was telling us the other day in class that a UNION is an ORGANIZATION that REPRESENTS teachers and their INTERESTS. I'm gonna ask again: What about MY interests??

But I kinda get the union thing. My dad is in one of them at the hospital where he works. He told me they protect workers from unfair bosses or whatever. But you know what? I'm pretty sure that the hospital union would probably make sure all them sick people were still taken care of, right? No matter what. Why don't this teachers' union make sure they teach??

Anyways, guess these unions are all worried about makin' sure teach is treated fair. And the union is worried because all these teachers need to be willing to

CHANGE. The unions were all moaning saying things about "job security" and teachers have a RIGHT and LONGEVITY which is when someone is there so long, nothing can happen to him. I have a question, tho', for those UNIONS. Where are my rights? Don't I have a RIGHT to be TAUGHT??? Don't I have a right to have a teacher that don't SLEEP in class?

But then everyone is saying if teach would not agree to the CHANGES, these teachers would be asked to MOVE ON. Some of those teachers just got on outta there. They knew. Ol' Mr. Hairless Legs Math Teach was one of the first to go. Everybody saying that he took his big ol' pension and was outta there for good at the end of the year. Pension. Ha. For sleeping and not working and not teaching and not caring and not not not not. Some of the others tried to hang on and insist on this or that, but bottom line is there were CHANGES happening. You were in or you were out. Kind of like a gang but on a whole other level.

Some of the teachers I felt kind of bad about. Some of them just did what they could to try and teach in the middle of the madness, but it was like, how are you supposed to teach when the building is burning down around you??? Anyway, some of those ok teachers were leaving too. I heard some of them talking, saying they were just sick of administrators coming and going and making this change and that change to try and improve things but the changes only lasted as long as the administrator was around or until the next election. So they were moving on VOLUN-TARILY to another school where they could just shut the door and teach in their own way without having to worry about new ways of doing things or whatever.

And some of those teachers leaving complained to anyone who would listen about, "this is ridiculous," and "why do I have to do this or do that to keep my job?" Huh. How do you feel about following rules that you don't like, that don't make sense to you, that you have no control over??? Huh? How does THAT feel???

In the middle of all this crazy talk, I kept going to class and making the motions. It was even harder tho' because man the teachers that didn't care before— well, they just got worse! I heard them saying stuff like this is why they don't try. Yeah right. Then the ones that did care, you could tell they were feeling the heat and the pain. Heard one of the good ones crying in the teachers' room that it was never about the kids. Gotta agree with her on that one.

And that's the way school year ended. All talk of change, but we will see. Yep, that was quite a first year for me at ol' Hope High!

CHAPTER 13

Over the summer, I tried to forget about that lame place, but the info was constant! Man, I could not get away from it. News about Hope was all over the place. You not gonna BELIEVE what happened!! Those teachers that didn't want to CHANGE, well! They was fired! A lot of them were at that school FOREVER. They were told they had to REAPPLY. That means that they had to ask for their job back. I couldn't believe it!

And day in and day out there was always news vans and reporters and photographers. Interviewing kids. That's the only time we've ever seen news reporters and camera people at our school. Except when there was a fight or a stabbing or arrest or some other stuff.

And then I hear they starting to build a CURRICULUM around SKILLS to make us JOB READY or COLLEGE READY or CAREER READY. A curriculum is kind of a map for education. What classes to take and in what order. There's so much excitement about all this I am afraid to hope that this time might be different. (Get it?! Afraid to HOPE.)

'N all of this because of this skinny little white dude and some Commissioner or somebody with a title like he should be in some Batman movie. Seems Hope really was hopeless and everybody saying "No Hope" and "Will There Be Hope?" 'n all that. Big time, right?

So all of a sudden there are these new people who are large and in charge directing this 'n that 'n writing out "expectations" 'n "setting objectives" 'n "aligning standards." 'N there was stuff on the TV on the local stations that Daddy like to watch when he gets home at night. Sometimes I sneak outta my room and snuggle up next to him just to be with him and smell him, and we watch the news 'til he pats my back and says get to bed. So I do, so I can be ready to go to that new school with all the "reform," but it's still Hope in a smelly old building.

But they do it. The state TAKES CONTROL of Hope High School and breaks it up into smaller schools of LEARNING COMMUNITIES. Art, info tech, and leadership. Leadership is where the kids go that want to be in the army. That's called ROTC. Art is for kids who like to draw or play guitar. Info tech is where I got put. I don't really know what that is, but I don't want art and I don't want ROTC, but it is a small LEARNING COMMUNITY so maybe teachers will teach 'n I will learn.

And some teachers are staying. Like Miz Anna and Dr. Ramirez. Do they actually care? Or do they not have the energy to move on? We'll see about that, now won't we?

CHAPTER 14

B ut, anyway, a lot was settled because in the fall, when we all
showed up at Hope, there was
these new people right at the door sayin'
stuff like "Welcome to Hope" and all that.
One thing I gotta say is the place was
clean. It even smelled better and looked
better, but we'll see. It's only the first day
and we'll see what happen to this place in
a week when the boys start writin' all over
the walls 'n taggin' the place.

We have this big assembly and now
there are three principals, not just one! For
the three schools inside that big old high

school. The big guy Dr. M be all talkin'
'bout learnin' communities and other ED-
UCATIONAL APPROACHES. Huh, we'll see
how much we learn.

Dr. M and Miss B and the SCHOOL
IMPROVEMENT TEAM are REBUILDING
Hope. The teachers that got hired 'n everybody all agreeing on this point and that
point. 'N they are gonna remake Hope High
School. REBUILD is what they keep saying. I keep saying why would you let a
teach sleep instead of teaching me? Start
there you crackers.

Mr. B 'n Mr. J 'n Mizz D 'n a couple
of others teach us about TECHNOLOGY.
What, do they think I'm stupid or something? I know TECHNOLOGY. I can write a
paper for school 'n check my email 'n use
a computer. But they are talking about re-
pairing computers 'n using PHOTOSHOP
'n getting CERTIFIED in MICROSOFT
PRODUCTS so I can get a JOB when I
GRADUATE.

And not only do they want all that,
they want to RESTORE ORDER and
TEACH 'N ENSURE SUCCESS OF EVERY

STUDENT. Huh. Excuse ME for not believin' that. They are always sayin' life is gonna get better 'n then it just don't. 'N then some other law is passed or some other POLITICIAN gets himself elected again or NOT 'n the changes for the good just keep stoppin' 'n startin' 'n stoppin' 'n startin' 'n stoppin' 'n startin'—this is my LIFE you crackers. I ain't no EXPERIMENT.

But I can't lie. There are changes happening at Hope. New computers are being delivered, 'n the graffiti is cleaned from the walls 'n doors. 'N there are even DOORS on the bathroom stalls! Is this time different? I'm almost afraid to hope.

CHAPTER 15

The first few days of tenth grade are kinda crazy 'n all. The kids that are used to running the place 'n leavin' class whenever they want 'n fightin' in the halls 'n wearin' gangsta colors are still trying to keep the place same old same old. But Dr. M 'n the other principals, they are out there in the halls keepin' order 'n maintaining CONTROL. Teachers too leave their rooms 'n stand outside class doors to welcome students. Say what?! I ain't never been welcomed into a CLASS before. But I like it. Most of the teachers even seem to mean it.

They don't seem to be afraid of leavin' the room to stand outside in the hall, neither. Before, teach leave the room, teach be ASKING for BIG trouble. Before the REBUILDING OF HOPE, one time teach stood outside the room 'n some of the boys got in there 'n shut the door on her so she was locked out of her own classroom. 'N they went through her purse 'n took money 'n then opened the window 'n climbed out. Them boys laughin' 'n laughin' so hard they couldn't even run. The teach, poor Miss L hollerin' 'n hollerin' for help 'n no one come to help. The other teachers just close their doors 'n don't help. Just ignore what was happening.

But it is different now. Seems like everybody is in agreement that nobody likes students being late and nobody likes graffiti and nobody likes tagging and on and on. 'N it seems that students are startin' to like it too as they stop taggin' 'n even come to class on time. 'N teachers seem to CARE. For real. 'N they all talk a lot about EDUCATION 'n how to deal with this educational challenge or that student's needs.

Like one time when I walked by this meetin' room where all the groups get together to discuss this and that. And there was some teachers arguing and getting all up in each other's faces about school work and policies and stuff. I guess some teachers let kids turn in work whenever the kids get it done. And I guess that sometimes means some kid did an entire quarter of work in like, three days. And they get to hollerin' and as I listen, I think does it matter that I didn't do it when you said I should do it? And if I can get all the sorry work done in three days then why don't you get up off of your sorry butt and give me work that takes me a while instead of your stupid assignments? "What did you do on your summer vacation?" Why, I parked myself by my in-ground pool and had my cabana boy bring me cocktails—stupid what did you think I did on my summer vacation? Sweated in my third floor tenement with nothing but the hot breeze from the cars on the freeway to cool myself. Stupid cracker.

But test scores are so low still even though Dr. M 'n the other principals have the teachers teach 'n teach 'n teach, but those tests 'r hard! Dr. M makes it as easy for us as he can—he gives us all snacks 'n stuff—but these tests are stressing everybody out. Some kids I know are just 'bout cryin' because they don't understand what is being asked.

Like, one of the science test questions was an article on the ocean 'n it keeps talking about sponges. What?! That is what I use on my dishes, what do you mean there's sponges in the ocean??

Then there's one on the ph in acid rain and its IMPACTS on lakes. I know what rain is 'n I know what acid is—didn't someone throw some of that in some whore's face once? But how is it raining acid? 'N what's ph? 'N how am I supposed to HYPOTHESIZE what to do about it when I don't know nothing and never been to no lake anyhow??

Everyone is all up in the principals' faces sayin we can't learn 'n what was the sense in wasting FUNDS on students that ain't gonna learn no how. Even people online all doom and gloom about ol' Hope

High. Discussing me like I ain't even there. This is my LIFE. You think maybe your TEST is all whacked? It ain't testin' what I know! 'N who decides what I should know? 'N who says I can't learn? You, Mr. Vanilla News Guy??? U ain't never even met me 'n you don't know me 'n you got no right to say I can't learn.

So even though there are BIG changes IMPLEMENTED, we're still not doing good on those tests.

But I'm learning! How come those tests don't measure that I can plan and TROUBLESHOOT and I'm getting ready to take these CERTIFICATION tests??? As I said, I'm in the IT Community so I get to go to my regular classes like English and Math, but then there's a whole bunch of special classes just for my community. Microsoft ones. Adobe ones. I didn't even know what Adobe was. I thought it was a pepper. I learn to do spreadsheets and mail merges and stuff. It is actually pretty cool. And I can edit photos in Adobe PRODUCTS. And I prepare for my certification tests so maybe if I want I can get a job right after high school. All this stuff is called SCHOOL TO WORK, SCHOOL TO CAREER, or SCHOOL TO COLLEGE. PATHWAYS to success.

They are all saying not everybody has to go to college. Which makes sense to me. Some people just ain't book smart. 'N they don't like sitting at a desk all day. 'N they don't like reading and reading and writing and writing and listening to teach talk 'n talk 'n talk 'n talk. Some kids just want to do stuff with their hands, like draw or play music or fix computers or work on computers. Message is all those courses and classes lead to WELL-PAYING jobs. Seems I might have a choice, after all.

We even have real computer labs and there is a computer for each one of us! We don't have to share! And most of the time they all work! Cool.

One of the new leaders of the IT Community tries to implement a helpdesk run by us kids. A helpdesk is one those places where you call if you need help with a computer. The idea is that students gain REAL WORLD experience doing jobs like that. Teach tried to set the class up so students would answer helpdesk calls for people in the building. You know, teach can't print. Student can't browse the web and is getting errors.

So the helpdesk is set up and kids are excited even if it is in a smelly old room down in the basement. Some fuzzy black stuff growing up the wall. And right near where the custodians take breaks. Those dudes smoke in there. Not supposed to because the school is a TOBACCO FREE ZONE, but they do anyways. Reeks! Between the cigarettes and the moldy stuff, the place is grim. But it is OURS. Our first project is to CONFIGURE the room and decide how we will greet customers. So we go about our business and it feels like there is a PURPOSE to stuff now. I can learn. I can help people. I can TROUBLESHOOT.

We drag in a couple of tables and some chairs and set up a computer to keep track of all our work and who we are helping. We even find a spare phone in a junk room and there's no phone jack in this grim room, but that's ok. We look around in all the other spaces to see if there is one that works that is not being used and we find one! It is a ways down the hall, but eh, what do we care? So we find a long telephone cord and have to string a couple of 'em together to make the cord reach our HELPDESK OF-FICE, but we do it. But, it is lying on the floor and teach says that ain't safe, someone might trip. Well, we want to make it safe so we talk to Mr. Roberto who is our supply guy. He's really nice and always helpful and he talks to us about ways to tape the cord so it isn't dangerous and he helps us out. Im-agine! We have a supply closet! That has supplies! And someone who will help us!

So we get ourselves all set up and teach lets us "RUN THE SHOW." We make decisions about MARKETING and COM-MUNICATION and determine WORKFLOW and ROLES and RESPONSIBILITIES and how to track our calls. Some of the kids in the Photoshop class help us design a logo with help from the Art Community and the kids in Microsoft Word class help us put together a brochure to advertise our ser-vices. Then the classes worked together to create the FINAL PRODUCT for our new helpdesk. We print in color using the color printer that WORKS! Then the database class helps us create a database so we can keep track of calls 'n our customers 'n problems. 'N we deliver our new brochure to all teachers' mailboxes! In all communities! Not just IT! So we are ready 'n we are in business! All of this is sooooo cool.

Minor stuff at first. Teach can't print. Kids can't access the internet. Did you know if it is just ONE kid that can't access the internet, it is probably just his computer? But if it is a whole class, then the problem could be SYSTEM WIDE.

Man, we were excited. Stuff was really happening. We were learning and responsible and teachers cared. The phone would ring and someone would say "I'm in this classroom at this computer and I've got this error," and they would read some number or message to us. And we got to decide based on SKILL SETS who should go to deal with this specific problem. And if there was more than one problem at a time and both problems were URGENT, how to PRIORITIZE.

And sometimes we could figure out the problems. DLL errors and stuff. Sometimes we couldn't, so we would have to get help from the central IT department. They didn't much like us at all because we were fixing stuff. Basic stuff, but we were still fixing problems.

And then the whole plan kind of exploded. Some of the IT staff at the central IT department filed a complaint with their UNION. Another union!? Are you kidding me?? Where's my union?? Why ain't there no UNION for students? Ain't I got rights??? A right to be TAUGHT? A right to be SAFE?? A right to LEARN??? Huh.

So the UNION got involved and said that a student-run helpdesk would take jobs away from the UNION staff. And they would file a GRIEVANCE if we CONTINUED IN THIS MANNER. And the school would be in trouble. How am I gonna take a job away from a UNION staff member when that computer has had a BROKEN sign on it for the last two months??? And no one came to fix it?? Huh? Explain that to me.

So the school and its brand new learning communities and new way of doing things seems to be shut down right at the beginning.

Kids and teach got pretty discouraged. We tried to keep doing little stuff to help the school and help our teachers and help other students, but there's only so much we can do without the MAN helping us out. Everything is locked so we can't even take a keyboard and clean it. UNION won't even allow spare keyboards or mice so we can do basic troubleshooting. Like we could SWAP OUT A KEYBOARD with another one to test. That's called PROBLEM DETERMINATION where if you got a keyboard that is not working, you gotta ask well, is it the keyboard or is it something else? Like the place on the back of the computer where the keyboard plugs in? That's called a PORT. One of the first steps you can do is you take a keyboard you know is working and plug it into the computer where the keyboard don't work. If the new keyboard works, then you are good to go! If the new keyboard don't work, then that's a whole other mess to figure out. Is it the port? You can try another port. It is cool trying to figure stuff out like that.

Anyway, we can't figure stuff out anymore 'cause they won't let us, so we walk around and organize cables behind desks because, man, whoever put that equipment there did not care at all about how things look or how things are organized. And someone donates a little vacuum cleaner to us. Did you know they make these special vacuum cleaners to vacuum computers? Who knew?? So we go around to the backs of all the computers and vacuum out the dust as that will help the computers last longer because the dust isn't getting sucked up inside and clogging everything up.

But union heard about that too and told us to stop. So now we sit in that smelly old room and the phone doesn't ring and we all look at each other and it is the longest saddest class imaginable. Teach finally pulls some CASE STUDIES together so we can read about how to solve problems and we have discussions about different AP-PROACHES to these problems and all of that is ok, but guess we are back to me IM-AGINING my education again. Sigh.

Then we have an idea that at least we could put all our spare equipment in our helpdesk that's not a helpdesk area. Then the equipment would be CENTRALIZED. That's important because then you can maintain INVENTORY of stuff and order more if you need it. We can't order stuff but we can at least get an idea of what we got. We don't got much 'cause the central IT department don't like us having anything, but it is something to do, so we do it.

But before we get started, some kid says we should clean and paint the place first to make it better. So we ask the custodian for cleaning stuff and they notify their union and we can't even CLEAN??? Are you KIDDING me??

We don't even bother trying to paint 'cause there's probably a union for painters too.

What I wanna ask all you UNION people is how is this helpful?? You work in a SCHOOL! Isn't it your job to put students first?!?! Oh, that's right. I forgot. This is public education. Public URBAN education. I almost had hope there for a minute.

Other classes are ok, though. We continue to work on earning the right to take the Microsoft Certification tests. Most of the computers still work. Some don't, though. Even though we FILE A HELPDESK TICKET with the downtown IT helpdesk, they sure take their sweet time getting here to help. Is it payback?? Maybe. We mostly just shrug it off. Same old, right? All those changes and same stupid man keeping the kids down.

There are other good stories, but the happy feeling around the opening of the new learning communities has kind of faded a bit. But life goes on, right?

CHAPTER 16

Like the time Hope won the state soccer championship. DIVISION I, everyone said. Guess that is the hardest division. Can't believe something like that happened. Poorest kids, some having to borrow sneakers. A mix of 'em all thrown together, not half of 'em even played together last year and they pulled it out. Nigerian kid led the team in scoring and all the players put him on their shoulders when he kicked the winning goal. Lots of people came out to see that game, but I heard some people were PISSED that the SUPERINTENDENT didn't even go. He's the one that STARTED the three learning communities and he didn't even come to the game. That is one sorry story right there.

But it was pretty cool—kids all high on their success and walking around proud. Proud of Hope. All of us wearing blue and cheering BLUE WAVE 'cuz that's what we are, you know the OCEAN STATE and waves and water and all that. Although I ain't never been to the beach here. Some people say it is nice.

CHAPTER 17

A nother time the boys' hoops team made it to the state championship. It was a different feeling to go to that gym at night and not be afraid of what was gonna happen. Lots of kids and families and even teachers came. It was safe and warm 'cuz the heat even worked and watching those boys hit those three pointers and win and win and win and everybody yelling BLUE WAVE and the cheerleaders going all rap and everybody proud.

So anyway the boys' hoops team fought and fought and had a winning season and even beat some of those private

schools to get to the finals. They were playing against a private school, some place
with a name like it is a country club or
something. I wonder how their NECAP
scores were?? I wonder if any of their fat
male math teachers just put their fat legs
up on the desk and sleep?? Huh. I can still
see that cat's white hairless chicken legs
up on the desk. Just about gives me the
shivers every time I think of that. Night-
mares, even.

Anyway, the finals were going to be
at a college gym to accommodate the
CROWDS that were expected. The principals even got us some buses, so as many
of us as wanted to could go down to that
big college campus and cheer for Hope.
And a bunch of us did—three buses were
full and everybody was excited and laughing and talking on the ride down. Principals even gave us all tix as they know some
of us couldn't pay. Got a little attitude from
the white guys collecting our tix looking us
up and down like we don't belong there,
but one thing we learned especially from
Miz Anna: it is all in how you CONDUCT

yourself. So we didn't give them all the sat-
isfaction of FULFILLING THEIR EXPECTA-
TIONS. We just kept being ourselves,
laughing and talking and being excited and
thanking Mr. Whitey when he gave us back
our half ticket stub.

Later on when we found our seats we
noticed a lot of people had a PROGRAM.
That's the paper that tells you who is playing and their numbers and everything.
None of us got one. Some of the kids got
pissed like they got dissed, like they
weren't important enough to get a program, so a few of 'em went back. I don't
know what all happened, but they came
back with a few and we shared.

But what's up with that? Why didn't
cracker give us a program? Seemed every
white person in that place was looking at a
program. Even the little kids who can't
even read hanging on to them and just
playing with them, flapping them up and
down. Sigh. This here is a special night and
somebody had to treat us like that??

But truth is we were kind of mad
nervous as none of us had been to a college

campus before. It was big and different but we did ok. Wish we woulda had money for snacks.

So the game started and we cheered and cheered and cheered, but you could tell Hope boys were just not as good as that fancy school. They played their hearts out and the game was exciting, but they lost. And at the end of the game, both teams had to stand in the center of the court and the losers got the second place trophies, and even though we cheer because they had nothing to be ashamed of it still felt bad. One those kids was so mixed up he was bawling right there on the court for everyone to see, and when they called his name to go up and get his trophy he lifted his shirt over his face so no one could see him crying, even though we all knew he was. Wasn't a dry eye in my section. We was all clapping, but our cheering was over and I had a big lump in my throat. But those boys tried and they gave everything on that court and they should be proud of that.

Sometime later I heard something very, very interesting about that star player on the winning team. His daddy was head basketball coach of the fancy college where that game was played. Heard that boy's daddy let that fancy school practice right on that same court where the championship game was. That can't be right. Ain't there a rule to prevent stuff like that from happening? Don't they have enough ADVANTAGE without getting MORE?? No wonder they won.

CHAPTER 18

Even tho' the school made all these changes, and it was much safer, we still had a SCHOOL RESOURCE OFFICER. That's a cop that is assigned to a school to keep control and arrest kids for crimes. Sarge Lyons. He's all right. I can't help but wonder why a cop gotta be in a school. Seems like the message is the place is more like a prison than a school. Is that the message you want to send??? But, there were some arrests. Just kids being kids and doing stupid kid stuff.

The school cop arrested a kid one day. Not sure what the kid did, but the cop arrested some kid and put the handcuffs on him and Sarge has to walk him through the hallways, and the kid is crying and screaming and just humiliated and Sarge just walks calmly behind. Sarge had a peaceful kind of way about him, just chill, and his eyes looked sad that he had to put a kid in handcuffs.

But then I got to know Sarge and got to understand better what he was trying to do. Build bridges, he said. That means connecting people in a good way, people that might normally fight. And he also said he liked to prevent problems before they blew up. How do you do that, anyway? How can you see a problem before it really becomes a problem? Wish I could have continued with that troubleshooting course. I wonder if we would have learned about problem prevention?

Sarge was ok for sure. He grew up in Providence and went to some of the same schools that have been labeled failing. Wish I had a chance to ask him how he did it. How did he come out of a failing school and find a good job?

CHAPTER 18

One time we got a mailing from some department in Providence School District. It was an ad for a workshop "My Child is an English Language Learner." The title and ad was in English only. Good one.

CHAPTER 20

I swear there were some kids that lived in that old school. There were some parts of the school that were closed off with locks. But we managed to get into some of the places. There was parts of a basement that were smelly and creepy. All moldy with barely a lightbulb. Creepy old place.

But, I knew these two brothers from Guatemala or some place in South America and they hated their home. Guess the father was a mean drunk and used to wail on them regular and so they never went home. Figured out a way to sneak around the security system and live at the school. They had heat during those bitter Rhode Island winters and could sneak leftovers outta the fridge in the cafeteria and even the faculty break room 'n had access to bathrooms and even the showers in the gym. So they did all right. But it must be something to not even want to go home because no one is taking care of you, or even worse, someone is beating you. I know for a fact that some of those teachers saw those brothers with bruises. You can tell a strap mark when you see it. And no one did anything. Aren't they supposed to REPORT ABUSE?!? But if they REPORT ABUSE, that means that somebody has to actually DO something. They have this whole department in this lame state that's supposed to take care of kids and families when there is abuse. I hear that department is almost as lame and as dysfunctional as the school system. Seems like there is always reports about some kid dying or being rushed to the hospital because some adult kicked or beat or hurt a kid. How can a grownup do that to a kid??

CHAPTER 21

I found out there was a guidance department at the school. Did not even know what that was. They're the people that are supposed to GUIDE you in "developing the skills necessary to realize your individual goals." Seriously. That's what the sign says. But the REALITY of the situation sure ain't THAT.

Oh sure, a couple of them counselors are ok, but some of 'em just ain't. First off, nobody but nobody told me about that office and nobody but nobody told me what they are supposed to be doing. They supposed to be helping me with my CAREER

PATH and how to NAVIGATE my choices, but I never had an appointment with NO-BODY in that department. And they got these nice offices, too! With desks they sit at and a couple of chairs in there for the so-called CLIENTS and all decorated with lamps and rugs and books. Looks nice, like a kid could just hang out in there all welcoming and all. But the reality is NOT. They don't care. Well, seems like most of 'em don't care. One does, though. He's an immigrant from Haiti or somewhere. An immigrant is someone who moves somewhere else to live. Mr. Obas is a cool guy. Always smiling and helping kids and giving advice. Like he's one of the ones that tried to help Nia when that cracker judge was trying to break her.

He makes me want to try and be better. What he went through to get out of his poor country and get to the USA, MAN what a story. He even speaks three languages and has lots of education. Did you know there's all kinds of education you can get? After high school? You can go for years! Guess that means you get paid more for them jobs. I didn't know that; all I knew was that there is a two-year college in RI and a couple of four-year colleges. But there are OPTIONS. Mr. Obas taught me that.

He is great. All this hate towards people who are not white or who are from another country, man what's up with that? Why you all hating on somebody like that? You look at somebody with skin darker or different from yours and speaks a little different, and you get all hateful. You don't know nothing about this person. Stop JUDGING. What is up with all you people JUDGING all the time???

But some of the other counselors in that office are LAME. I had to meet with one of them to discuss my CAREER PATH. Old white lady, she's in a sweet little office nothing like her. She is one cold, hard lady. Face all pinched up like she is bitter or sucking on lemons. I hear her tell kids all the time that they, "just aren't college material." She is judging this by looking at our GRADES. What is up with you all judging me just on grades?! I got motivation and smarts and want to have a CAREER, but am held down by the SYSTEM of unions and teachers that don't care and don't measure me for nothing but how many things I got right or wrong.

I try not to go to her because she judges and because she always looking like she got a bad taste in her mouth and wants to spit it out whenever she talks to me. Won't listen to me or nothing. Isn't part of counseling to listen?!!?

The nicest lady in that department is the secretary, or ADMINISTRATIVE ASSISTANT. Miss Patricia was nice to everybody, every time we would go to the office. Always calling everybody "dear," but in a nice way like you knew she meant it. She was a little thing and kind of old, but she was still alright, you know? She would even pat your arm if she thought you was upset. She probably would have patted our shoulders, but she was so tiny, she couldn't reach that high. Anyway, she got sick. Next thing you know, she just wasn't feeling right. Even started saying it out loud to people. And she never complained, that one. She kept kind of holding her belly and saying she felt sick. She finally went to the doctor's and she had cancer and never came back to school and died in like a week. That's some sad stuff right there. I'll miss her.

CHAPTER 22

One of the new things we had to do for graduation included a PORT-FOLIO PRESENTATION. We had to collect EXEMPLARS which are examples of our good work over the course of our HIGH SCHOOL CAREER and present to teachers and other students and even the news was going to be there. That might be a PROBLEM because I ain't got no EXEMPLARS. But I'm only in tenth grade, so maybe there is time. And maybe there might be HOPE because now teachers are teaching! I might get me some EXEMPLARS after all!

I wanted to go to some of those portfolio presentations to see what I was in for, so

I did. There were OPEN to all. I went to see a girl's presentation. She was named Jayplo which means Beautiful Girl. She talked about what she had learned and how she had grown as a person. And she was beautiful, with long legs and big butt. Man, some guys love a lot of junk in the trunk. But she was raped during some wars and violence in her country. I don't know if it was Sierra Leone or Liberia but somewheres in Africa. But she had a baby boy and she talked about what it was like to come to this country with a baby and not knowing any English and having to learn all that and then pass some test that some people said she had to pass to prove something. She named her baby boy Wonlay Tehpoe which she says means "tired" and "I am not to be blamed." It is cool when names mean something like that. People ask me all the time what is up with "Seaira" and I say it is just some name my mother liked so shut your mouth. And what is a name, anyway? Like my friend Nieve; her mother named her for "snow" even though that girl is black, but I guess it was snowing when Nieve came in to this world.

CHAPTER 23

So life is really changing. Kids are going to class and teachers are teaching and there's no more graffiti and there is even soap and doors on the stalls in the restrooms! During those times when teaching and learning is happening, there ain't but nobody in the hallways. Quite the change. I'm not even really afraid anymore. Well, most times I'm not. Cause they'se still some chuckle-heads that will do something stupid or even serious.

Like one time, somebody smuggled a gun in. See, we have to go through these metal detectors to try and catch kids that'll sneak in knives or guns or whatever. They say they need to protect themselves and I believe that 'cause there is still some GANG ACTIVITY around. Even tho' there ain't no graffiti and you don't see no gang tags, they still around. Tattoos on their arms and the way they shake each other's hands and nod at each other. But for the most part, the principals are demanding a SAFE EN-VIRONMENT that is CONDUCIVE to learning. So, we go through metal detectors.

But, there are always ways around that, see? You can leave a gun on an outside windowsill in a brown paper bag so it looks like trash or whatever, and then get it during the day. Just slide on up to the window, open it up, grab the bag and slide onto your seat or out the door to your classroom. Or, you can toss a gun or a knife to somebody who catches it. And that's what happened. One kid had some issues with another kid and, bam, just like that, somebody is tossing a gun up to the first floor window in a classroom and some teach sees it and they call for Sarge to come. And the gun is confiscated and both kids are arrested and everyone is kind of relieved that everything happened the way it is supposed to happen, you know what I mean? A grownup actually saw an INCIDENT and reported it and everything was ok. Except that those two kids? The two that got arrested for smuggling the gun on to school grounds? They got kicked out of school. Lotta people saying yeah, that's right—they brought a gun to school and they DESERVE to be kicked out. But I got two questions over that. First, what's gonna happen to those kids that caused the problem to begin with? They're from another neighborhood and don't even go to school and they're the ones bothering Hope kids while they trying to get themselves an EDUCATION. I ain't heard nothing about them. And the second question is what's those two Hope kids supposed to do now? Huh? Their future is RUINED when they was just trying to protect themselves and didn't know where else to turn. What's gonna happen to them? They can't go to school no more. They're probably going to spend time in jail. Ain't got no future at all now, probably. All about stuff that is just out of their control.

I guess it is still a city. An URBAN school with all its CHALLENGES.

CHAPTER 24

Must be a challenge still to teach. No matter all the changes made. It sure is challenging for me to learn. But sometimes, teachers just make it fun. There's this one teach who likes to do an EGG DROP CHALLENGE. Kids get to design and build these crates or whatever to protect the egg if it is dropped from a tall building. It is all about FORCE and AC-CELERATION and GRAVITY. Seems like this is the first time some of us got a chance to do some HANDS-ON activities. So we all build these crates using styrofoam or whatever. And teach takes 'em all up to the top of the school. Kids couldn't go up because it was too dangerous, but we all watched from below. And we had DATA SHEETS where we had to record what happened to try and figure out a better way. You should have seen it. Man, it was great. Kids all excited 'bout learning. Laughing and talking and some even playing music on their phones. And the teach dropping eggs in their special designed packaging off the roof of that school. Kids were so fired up and making so much noise, some of the people came out of the houses all around just to see what the excitement was. It was awesome to see. People that before wouldn't say two words to us were talking and laughing with us and asking questions. Pretty cool day. My egg got crushed, though. I think I have an idea to make it better. Wonder if teach will let us REVISE our WORK??

CHAPTER 25

Another time, it was after school and some kids were just hanging out in the halls. Maybe they didn't have anywhere to go. Or maybe they just actually LIKED being at school! Imagine that. Anyway, they were sitting around at the end of the long hallway talking and laughing. Then they started singing. Six boys. All of 'em with voices that sounded like they should be in the church choir. It was just beautiful. I ain't never said that before—something at the school was beautiful. Anyway, a couple of teachers came by to listen and applaud and the boys were just liking the attention. You could see it in their eyes and faces. Somebody was giving them attention for their TALENTS. Then the weirdest thing happened. This assistant principal came out of his office which was right near where the boys were singing and hollered at them to stop. Now why would he do that? Kids having fun, not causing any trouble or problems and this mean little AP comes out and just pisses all over it. I could see the hurt in their faces for one split second before their whole faces closed off and their eyes just shut down. Man, that was sad. Even the two teachers who was listening to the boys sing and encouraging them, they couldn't believe it either. They looked at each other with this look on their faces like "WHAT???" I was hoping they would do or say something to that little mean guy, but nope. Guess he was their boss or something.

CHAPTER 26

Even though stupid stuff happens like that every day, the school seems to be getting better. More positive. Kids liking to come to school. Seems like the teachers do too.

The school is even more open to visits from families. Guess a couple of teachers went and did some research. Trying to understand why hardly anybody came to open houses. An open house is where families can come and meet teachers and learn about the school. That's a cool idea, right? Ain't never had one before at Hope. So they tried, but no one showed up. These teachers wanted to figure out what was wrong, why nobody came.

After doing the RESEARCH, them teachers learned that these families find the school UNWELCOMING. I mean, I get that—it is a big building with four floors and bars on the windows and kind of looks like a hospital or prison or something. Not friendly at all. Not sure why them teachers needed to do RESEARCH to find out that families find the place a little scary. Isn't it obvious??? You got families that can't speak English, they mostly from little towns in Latin America, are new to the country....Yo, you think they're really gonna come to an open house?

So, the ADMINISTRATION decided to change the way it OPERATES. They did a bunch of things that just made it better. They made sure all the invites were in a bunch of different languages. They asked kids to translate and conduct tours in their NATIVE LANGUAGE. They even arranged to serve some food! For this first open house was called FAMILY NIGHT and they served spaghetti and meatballs! And some

people knew some people and next thing
you knew, there was a salsa band performing right in our cafeteria! Somebody even
delivered apples from a nearby orchard!
Imagine that! Those apples were so good.
Wow they tasted different than the ones I
buy in the store. The ones I buy in the store
are a little mushy sometimes. And some
other people decorated and it looked nice.
That old cafeteria looked nice.

And families came! All dressed up.
The admins left the doors to the school
WIDE OPEN so people would feel welcome!
And students stood out front welcoming
families. Moms and dads and aunts and
uncles and sisters and brothers and gram-
mies and grandfathers came! It was something. Everybody eating and laughing and
dancing. Some people trying to teach that
grumpy little AP how to dance. White people just can't move is all I'm saying. But it
was a real good time. Real good.

So it is all POSITIVE, right? I'm liking my classes in the new IT SMALL
LEARNING COMMUNITY. I am LEARNING
stuff! Adobe PRODUCTS and MICROSOFT

stuff. I can MANIPULATE data and I'm learning about JOBS that REQUIRE these SKILLS! I mean, we still can't repair anything because of that UNION ISSUE, but still. Learning's learning, right? Gotta take what you can take!

And who knew that there's supposed to be a CURRICULUM that schools and teachers follow? Like, I'm in tenth grade and I gotta take all these courses about English and Math and stuff, but also all that computer stuff. And if I take an Intro course—that means INTRODUCTION—this year, I can take another one next year that is a little more advanced. Cool. And then I can work for my CERTIFICATIONS and get a JOB right after high school. Or maybe even over the summer!! Or maybe I can go to COLLEGE and choose to CONTINUE MY EDUCATION. I almost can't believe it. Sometimes I look around my classroom and want to pinch myself to be sure I am not dreaming. Why was I so lucky???

But I got something to say about luck. Why does a kid have to be LUCKY to get an education in Providence??? Or anywhere? I mean, I didn't get into Classical, but I could have been sent to Mount Pleasant or Central. Man, I got friends over in those places and they got some STORIES to tell. Remember ol' white legs? Snoring in class? Paper said he retired but, he CAME OUT OF RETIREMENT. Yeah, they just moved his sorry old self over to Central. He's sleeping through more classes and NOT BEING HELD ACCOUNTABLE. What is UP with that, I ask you?? I have to be HELD ACCOUNTABLE every damn day. Why not him? Huh? Why not him?

CHAPTER 27

There's still a lot of good stuff at ol' Hope. All those classes I was taking that was about Microsoft and Adobe? The school got some money from some grant that was gonna pay for our CERTIFICATION TESTS, right? A grant is when someone gives money to pay for something. Not like for me to buy a car although that would be great, but to support a school or whatever. Anyways, a bunch of students QUALIFIED to take the tests! See, there's this whole process where to be CERTIFIED in something means to meet a certain STANDARD that a company or industry sets. Microsoft and Adobe said we had to prove we could do certain things to earn the right to be certified.

So teach has been showing us and we've been practicing and now we get to take the tests! To prove what we know! We had to register and everything with IDs and that was kind of a pain 'cause some of the kids didn't have no ID, but teach helped us get it all worked out and we were all registered to take the tests.

The day of the tests came and everybody was all nervous, but teach and the principal said we could do it. They gave us snacks 'cause they know some of us ain't had nothing to eat for breakfast and made sure the room was quiet and all. We had to take the tests online. That means not on paper but on the computer. And we did. It took a long time and teach couldn't answer any questions or help us, but he gave advice like read the question carefully. And sometimes the test asked us to show what we would do. It was a like a Microsoft program that was inside the test. I wonder how they did that. Like I had to INSERT AND RESIZE A PHOTO in a document and add page numbers and stuff. And I did! I knew how to do all that!

At the end of the test was a SUBMIT button, and I did. I submitted my test and got my score right away. Some kind of computer program graded it right there! I passed! Pretty much everybody in the class did, too. And everybody was happy and proud and teach got an email from Microsoft with our certificates and there's a color printer right in the classroom so we printed out the certificates and there was a line for teach to sign and he did! The certificate said I passed the FUNDAMENTALS test. Cool. Next I can take ASSOCIATE level then EXPERT. Then maybe I can get a job!

What's great about all this is that part of learning about Microsoft and Adobe is the careers that are out there! A career is more than a job, it is a choice to PURSUE something that interests you. I like IT. And you know, people can make some good money knowing all IT stuff?

The other thing that is pretty cool is that I am now thinking about my future! I have a future. In IT.

CHAPTER 28

In April, we get the word that a company is recruiting us. That means that the company is interested in hiring us for actual JOBS for the summer! Man, everybody is talking about that. Imagine, having some place to go during the summer where I can learn more AND earn money!!

So teach works with this company to set up interviews and he talks to us about how to apply. Like when teachers had to apply for their jobs at Hope, but different! We fill out application forms and we know not to make mistakes because the company won't hire someone who is careless, so I fill mine out real careful like and turn it in. And sure enough, I get called for an interview. It is during the school day, but teach and the principal are ok with that because this is what everybody's been working for, right?

Teach works with us on interview skills so we are ready to SELL OUR-SELVES. We even start to put together our portfolios so we can show EXEMPLARS of our work.

I have never been more ready for this interview.

I nail it.

I get offered a job.

And suddenly all this is real. The changes. The hope. My future.

CHAPTER 24

I work hard over the summer at my job because I want to establish a good track record and a good reputation as a good worker. That's what teach says. Always do a good job. Because I can then use this job to get a better one. So I do. I do a good job. I listen and learn and I go through all the training and do my job at a helpdesk. Just doing basic stuff, but imagine how much better I could be if I had the chance at Hope to really work at that school helpdesk?

And that's my summer. Now I have something to write when teach asks how I spent my summer vacation.

CHAPTER 30

Eleventh grade starts out pretty good. We're all excited to be back. I get to take advanced courses to prepare myself for those additional tests so I can move from basic to associate to expert certifications in Microsoft. And Adobe, too! There's levels of certifications for that, too. Those programs are hard, but I can do it. I know I can. I got a good teacher and the computers work and we have all the software we need.

The other thing about the eleventh grade—you are not going to believe this. You know that NECAP test? Well! Seems like the whole school did so much better than the other times we took it! I don't really understand it all, but there are LEVELS of PROFICIENCY and they measure us in PERCENTAGES as in what PERCENTAGE passed or are proficient. Proficient means how good somebody is at something. And the school did pretty good.

Everybody celebrated THAT, let me tell you. People smiling and laughing and there was a lot of hugging and principals even had a little party in the caf. Just soda and cake, but still. A party to celebrate our success.

See? We can learn. We can succeed. All we needed was a chance.

But then we start to hear stuff that none of us like at all.

CHAPTER 31

All of a sudden they got some new politico somewhere who hired a new top dog who is in charge of all them schools. First thing he does?? Cuts funding for Hope. That means they take money away from us. Can't afford to DEVOTE so many RESOURCES to just one school, he says.

Those cuts? Yeah, you know what that means. They use the term SLASH a lot. Like slashing tires but different. This time it is our hopes and dreams they are SLASHING.

They SLASH staffing. Some of those teachers? Gone. Just like that. Right in the middle of the school year.

They SLASH other stuff, too. All those certification tests? Nope. No more money for those.

Everybody walking around like they had their hearts ripped out. Some teachers are crying. Kids are crying too. All of us sayin' what was the point???

They get rid of the ROTC community. Seems like these new politicos don't like the idea of preparing kids to go to WAR. ROTC is more than that! Can't you see??? It is about LEADERSHIP and just 'cause ROTC is part of the army or whatever doesn't mean kids are gonna go fight in a war!!

And if this is all about CAREERS, well the ARMY is a good career! I met somebody once at the school with all kinds of ribbons on his chest and he told me he makes A LOT of money. And there are different careers in the army. Not every one of 'em involves a GUN or WAR!!

And, I'm pretty sure you all knew you shoulda thought about paying for all of this when you started. So why, huh? Whydja START if you knew you couldn't FINISH??

And the other thing that just ain't right is the COST. All of these changes COST something, right? Don't you think it is going to COST to rip it all apart? And rebuild it? AGAIN?

So here I am, in my junior year, ready to continue my CAREER PATH and all of a sudden there's no money. None. Where'd all that go, anyways? Wasn't it just there?? Where's the money for my certification tests?

All of this is so awful that I don't know what's worse. Is it worse that you got my HOPE up and then let it down? Is that worse than being HOPELESS to begin with? Or is it worse that now my brother ain't got nothing to look forward to at all? That he ain't got no HOPE in his future??

ABOUT THE AUTHOR

Marie F. Beardwood is a native Rhode Islander. She graduated from St. Raphael Academy in Pawtucket, Rhode Island, earned her teaching credential in English Secondary Ed from Rhode Island College and her master's degree from Columbia University Teachers College in New York. She has dedicated her career to ensuring excellence in education in public and private sectors in K-12 and higher ed throughout Southern New England, Brazil, and South Korea.

Marie loves vintage jewelry and vintage pocketbooks, the kettle ponds and oceans of Cape Cod, Massachusetts, the woods of Chepachet, Rhode Island, fur coats, her strong and amazing women friends, and her husband of 35 years. Not necessarily in that order.

Visit her website: www.MarieFBeardwood.com.